Fiddlesticks

Beverly Lewis

Beverly Lewis Books for Young Readers

PICTURE BOOKS

Annika's Secret Wish • *In Jesse's Shoes*
Just Like Mama • *What Is God Like?*
What Is Heaven Like?

THE CUL-DE-SAC KIDS

The Double Dabble Surprise
The Chicken Pox Panic
The Crazy Christmas Angel Mystery
No Grown-ups Allowed
Frog Power
The Mystery of Case D. Luc
The Stinky Sneakers Mystery
Pickle Pizza
Mailbox Mania
The Mudhole Mystery
Fiddlesticks
The Crabby Cat Caper
Tarantula Toes
Green Gravy
Backyard Bandit Mystery
Tree House Trouble
The Creepy Sleep-Over
The Great TV Turn-Off
Piggy Party
The Granny Game
Mystery Mutt
Big Bad Beans
The Upside-Down Day
The Midnight Mystery

Katie and Jake and the Haircut Mistake

www.BeverlyLewis.com

THE CUL-DE-SAC KIDS

Fiddlesticks

•

Beverly Lewis

BETHANY HOUSE PUBLISHERS
MINNEAPOLIS, MINNESOTA 55438

Fiddlesticks
Copyright © 1997
Beverly Lewis

Cover illustration by Paul Turnbaugh
Story illustrations by Janet Huntington

Published by Bethany House Publishers
11400 Hampshire Avenue South
Bloomington, Minnesota 55438

Bethany House Publishers is a division of
Baker Publishing Group, Grand Rapids, Michigan.

Printed in the United States of America

ISBN   978-1-55661-911-3

Library of Congress Cataloging-in-Publication Data

Lewis, Beverly.
    Fiddlesticks / Beverly Lewis.
        p.   cm. — (The cul-de-sac kids ; 11)
    Summary: Even though rotten Ronny torments Shawn
with a mean nickname, Shawn practices the Golden Rule.
ISBN 1-55661-911-1 (pbk.)
    [1. Nicknames—Fiction. 2. Behavior—Fiction.
3. Korean Americans—Fiction. 4. Christian life—Fiction.]
I. Title. II. Series: Lewis, Beverly. Cul-de-sac kids ; 11.
PZ7. L58464Fi   1996
[Fic]—dc21   96–45852
                                          CIP
                                          AC

For Michael,
a soccer-lovin'
fan,
who eagerly awaits
the new books
in this series.

THE CUL-DE-SAC KIDS

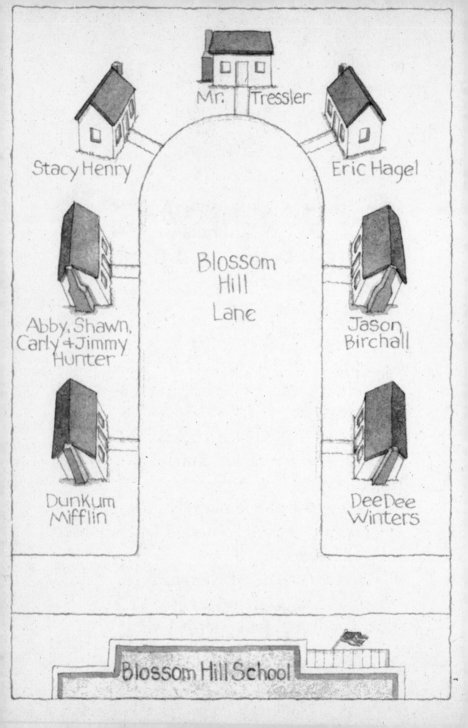

ONE

Shawn Hunter tuned his violin.

"Ready to practice?" his American sister asked.

"Almost." Shawn tucked the violin under his chin. He smiled at Abby. "Now ready."

Abby held the music. "High enough?"

"Very good," Shawn said. It came out like *velly* good.

Shawn was still learning to speak English. His first language was Korean. Abby's parents had adopted him.

It was hard getting used to a new country. And a new school. But music lessons weren't new. Shawn, whose Korean name was Li Sung Jin, loved music. Mostly violin music.

"I start now," Shawn said.

He drew the bow across the strings. A soaring melody filled the living room.

Abby tapped her toe to the music.

Suddenly, Shawn stopped playing.

"What's wrong?" asked Abby.

"Something missing," Shawn said.

He set his violin and bow on the sofa. He hurried down the hall to his bedroom.

Soon, he returned with his soccer ball.

"What's *that* for?" Abby asked.

"Ball help balance me," Shawn said.

He picked up his violin and bow. He set his right foot on top of the soccer ball. "That better."

Abby giggled.

Shawn began to play again.

He practiced major scales. Next he reviewed two old songs. He worked on two new ones.

Over and over he practiced. Shawn loved playing his violin. As much as he loved playing soccer.

Shawn liked to dribble and punt. Sometimes he practiced in his big backyard. Mostly when no one was watching.

Practicing in secret wasn't easy. But Shawn was determined to play with the Blossom Hill Blitzers. The team was named for Shawn's school. He wasn't sure what Blitzers meant. But it sounded good. Fast too.

★ ★ ★

When Shawn finished practicing his violin, Abby clapped. "You sound double dabble good!" she said.

"Thank you." Shawn gave a stiff bow.

Woof!

Abby looked at their dog, Snow White.

"What's the matter with you?" she asked the floppy-eared pet.

Shawn laughed his high-pitched laugh. "Snow White not like violin music."

"Bad dog," Abby scolded. She went over and tickled her paws. She was lying on her back. All four legs were sticking up. "Shawn makes nice music," she told Snow White. "You don't have to play dead."

Shawn was still laughing. "Snow White need music lesson. She not understand."

"You're right," Abby said. She put the music away.

Shawn stopped laughing. Now he spoke softly. "Some *people* not understand, too."

"What?" Abby asked.

"Is not important," Shawn muttered into his violin case.

Abby insisted. "What did you say?"

Shawn was silent.

He put his violin away. *Snap!* The lid clicked shut.

Abby sat on the floor and touched Shawn's arm. "Something's bugging you," she said. "You can't fool me."

Shawn sat beside her. "Abby good sister and *chingu*."

"Friends talk to each other," Abby said.

Shawn sighed. His dark, almond-shaped eyes grew serious. He pushed his hand through his black hair.

"I not fit in. America hard place for Korean kid. With violin," he added quickly.

"It takes time getting used to a new culture. But don't give up," Abby pleaded. She looked at him. "Are kids at school making fun of you?"

Shawn nodded sadly. "They have nickname for me."

Abby frowned. "What are they calling you?"

Shawn's eyes popped open. "Abby mad?"

"Yes, I'm mad!" She stood up. "What's the nickname?"

"They say make-fun name," he said. "They say, 'fiddlesticks.' Because I skinny and . . . and small. And play violin. Boys not play violin in America?"

"Of course they do," Abby said. She puffed air through her lips. "Who's calling you fiddlesticks?"

"Kids who not like me," Shawn said.

Abby nodded. "I figured that, but who?"

"I not say." Shawn got up and walked toward the kitchen.

"Hey, come back!" Abby called.

But Shawn didn't answer. He couldn't. There was a big lump in his throat.

TWO

The next day was Friday, March first.

Miss Hershey made an announcement to the class. "Today is the beginning of Music in Our Schools Month."

Shawn grinned. "Very good," he whispered.

Abby smiled at him across the row.

Shawn thought, *Music month great idea*.

Miss Hershey talked about composers. Famous ones. "The Three B's," she called them. Bach, Beethoven, and Brahms.

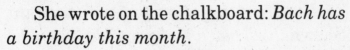

She wrote on the chalkboard: *Bach has a birthday this month*.

"Who knows when this composer was born?" the teacher asked.

Shawn sat up straight. "Yes!" he said. "1685, very long time."

Miss Hershey smiled. "Thank you, Shawn. That's correct. March 21, 1685. A long time ago, indeed." She wrote the date on the board.

While her back was turned, some kids made faces at Shawn. "Fiddlesticks," they said.

Abby heard.

So did Miss Hershey. "No talking, please!"

Shawn slumped in his seat. He couldn't help being small and thin.

He stared at Miss Hershey's desk. There was a suggestion box at one end. Miss Hershey emptied the box every Thursday. She read the suggestions to the class, and they discussed each one.

I write suggestion for box, thought Shawn. *I tell teacher about make-fun kids*.

Miss Hershey walked to her desk. "Class, please open to page 57 in your language arts notebook," she said. "We will work till recess."

Shawn looked in his desk. He found a notebook and pencil. He began to write his name on the seat-work page.

"Ps-st—fiddlesticks!" someone whispered.

It was Ronny Kitch, the boy behind him.

"Hey, fiddlesticks boy," Ronny whispered again.

Shawn refused to turn around.

Ronny tapped Shawn's shoulder. "What page are we supposed to do?" he asked.

Slowly, Shawn turned. He was going to be nice. He was going to give Ronny the page number.

But now Ronny was making his eyes

slant. He was pulling at his eyes on purpose. Making fun of Shawn. "Only a sissy plays a fiddle," Ronny hissed through his teeth.

In a flash, Shawn turned back around. He was *not* a sissy!

Instead of starting on the assignment, Shawn pulled out a fresh piece of paper. He glanced at Miss Hershey's suggestion box.

He wrote: *I not like to tattle. Students call me name. Name is Fiddlesticks. Because I short, little person. Because I come from Korea and play violin.*

Shawn read what he'd written. Then he picked up his pencil again.

I make suggestion for box. Can teacher make name stop? I thank you very much.

Respect to you,

Shawn Hunter—Li Sung Jin,

from Korea

Shawn folded the note and pushed it into his jeans. Before recess, he would visit the suggestion box.

"Hey, fiddlesticks boy," Ronny said in his ear. "What do you think you're doing?"

Shawn froze.

Had Ronny seen the note?

THREE

Ronny Kitch raised his hand. He waved it high.

"Yes, Ronny?" Miss Hershey said.

"I need to speak to you," he said.

Miss Hershey called him to her desk. They were whispering. Ronny shook his head. Then he turned and pointed to Shawn.

Miss Hershey's eyebrows flew up. "Shawn Hunter?" she said.

Quickly, Shawn stood up and bowed.

The kids snickered.

But Miss Hershey was kind. "In America, we don't bow when someone speaks to us," she explained. "Do you understand?"

Shawn nodded. He almost forgot and started to bow again.

"Will you please see me at recess?" the teacher asked.

Shawn nodded again. "I come see you."

He sat down, worried. What had Ronny just told Miss Hershey?

Shawn thought and thought. He *had* been fooling around, not doing his seat work. Was Miss Hershey going to talk to him about *that*?

Ronny marched down the row of desks. He bumped against Shawn on the way back to his seat. He shoved him hard on purpose.

Miss Hershey was too busy to notice.

Shawn didn't like being pushed around. But he was a peanut next to Ronny. His arm muscles were like three jelly beans. His legs were like toothpicks.

Or . . .

Shawn swallowed the lump in his throat.

He looked down at his legs. They looked like violin bows. Like fiddlesticks.

No wonder the kids called him that!

Shawn sighed. He hoped Ronny wouldn't pick a fight. Even if Shawn wanted to fight, he couldn't beat him. Ronny was tough. He was mean.

Determined not to slouch, Shawn picked up his pencil. He read the assignment and began to fill in the answers.

Abby glanced over at him. Her lips formed these words: *Are you OK?*

Shawn rubbed his nose. He formed these words back: *Shawn OK.*

But he wasn't. Not really.

Abby turned her head and went back to work.

So did Shawn.

When he was finished, he took out a book about soccer. Miss Hershey wanted everyone to keep a library book handy. She called it free reading—when you finished seat work early.

Shawn liked books. He was a good reader. And smart. He wished he could talk better. Faster too.

The soccer book was exciting. From the time he'd learned to walk, Shawn liked to kick a ball around.

And two weeks from now, Shawn wanted to try out for the Blitzers. But he wanted to watch the boys practice *today*.

Then he remembered. His violin lesson was after school. What could he do?

Shawn stared at the pictures in the soccer book. He thought about Ronny. Would *he* be at soccer practice?

Shawn stopped thinking and started reading. The soccer book was wonderful. He couldn't stop reading.

Soon, ideas were bouncing in his head. Maybe he could watch practice after violin lesson. Maybe he wouldn't be too late getting home.

He wished he could practice out on the soccer field. He was tired of practicing in secret. The backyard was OK. But the gigantic soccer field—that would be terrific!

Kids could dribble, punt, and kick on a field like that. They could guard and do teamwork. Soccer stuff—things that made a great player.

Eric Hagel and Jason Birchall were good players, too. They were two of Shawn's best friends. Eric and Jason lived on his street, a cul-de-sac. It was called Blossom Hill Lane, close to Blossom Hill School.

Eric, Jason, and Shawn belonged to The Cul-de-sac Kids. Nine kids on one street. Each one was Shawn's *chingu*— friend!

He was glad for friends. Very glad.

Then he remembered rotten Ronny Kitch.

He not chingu, Shawn thought.

Shawn closed the soccer book. He felt scared thinking about Ronny. *I forget about soccer team*, he thought. *I not try out*.

The recess bell rang.

Time to see Miss Hershey.

Shawn stood up. Slowly, he went to the front of the classroom.

"You see me, yes?" he asked.

"Let's talk," Miss Hershey said. "Have a seat."

Just then, Ronny ran outside for recess. Shawn could hear him laugh. It was a loud laugh. A roaring laugh.

Shawn sat near Miss Hershey's desk. She looked him in the eyes.

Shawn bit his lip.

Was he in big trouble?

FOUR

Miss Hershey's voice was soft. "Were you passing notes in class?"

"No pass note," Shawn said.

Miss Hershey asked, "Did you write one?"

Shawn was worried. Ronny *had* seen him.

He reached into his jeans pocket. The note for the suggestion box was all folded up. He handed it to Miss Hershey.

Her eyes opened wide. "What's this?" she asked.

Shawn said, "This what I write in class. So sorry." It sounded like so *sallee*.

The teacher opened the note. Her pretty blue eyes scanned the page.

She looked up. "My goodness," she said. "You don't deserve a nickname, Shawn. Thank you for telling me about this."

He nodded his head in a half bow. Then he caught himself. "Sorry."

Miss Hershey's smile was warm. "Please, don't be bashful about talking to me. I want all my students to feel comfortable at school. Always."

Shawn said, "Thank you," and headed outside.

Several boys were already playing soccer. Ronny Kitch was on the field, too.

Shawn stood beside the swings and watched.

Abby ran over to him. "What did Miss Hershey want?"

Shawn said, "We have talk. Miss Hershey very nice teacher."

"I know that," Abby insisted. "But why'd she want to see you?"

Shawn explained about the suggestion box. And about his note.

Abby's eyes started to get shiny in the corners. "Did you tell her who is calling you 'fiddlesticks'?"

Shawn looked down at his feet. "I not say."

Abby shook her head. "Come on, Shawn, you have to tell her!"

Shawn's eyes were wet, too. He wanted them to be dry. But they kept getting watery.

Shawn ran into the school—right to the boys' room. He washed his face.

Soon, Eric came in, too. He stared at Shawn's face. "You've been crying," he said. "What's wrong?"

"Nothing wrong." Shawn looked away.

"Something *is* wrong!" Eric said.

Just then, Ronny Kitch burst in the door.

Shawn saw him first. He didn't say anything to Ronny. He darted past him and ran into the hallway.

At the drinking fountain, Shawn's heart was pounding.

And quickly, he rubbed his eyes dry.

FIVE

At lunch, Shawn sat with Abby and her friend, Stacy Henry.

Dunkum Mifflin, another Cul-de-sac Kid, came over and sat with them.

Eric and Jason were having hot lunch. They joined Shawn, Abby, and the others.

Shawn and Abby had their packed lunches from home. Shawn used chopsticks to eat cold *bulkoki* in a plastic dish. He'd sprinkled garlic on the sticky rice this morning. Bulkoki was his favorite lunch.

Shawn held up his cold Korean stir fry. "OK with you?" he asked everyone at the table.

Eric and Jason didn't seem to mind.

Dunkum pinched his nose just for fun.

Stacy Henry smiled. "It's OK."

Shawn always asked his American friends about the garlic smell. It was the kind thing to do.

"Why'd you run away in the boys' room?" Eric asked.

Shawn's mouth was full. He didn't answer.

When he finished chewing, Ronny Kitch had shown up.

"AAUGH!" Ronny covered his nose. "What's that horrible smell?"

Abby grinned. "It's garlic. And if it bugs you, then go away."

"YUCK! Garlic isn't cool," he roared at Shawn. "Haven't you learned anything about America?"

Eric and Jason looked at each other.

Their mouths dropped open.

Stacy shook her head.

Dunkum frowned.

Abby did, too.

Shawn put his head down. He was afraid. Ronny might hit him. Maybe smash his teeth in or something worse.

He stared at his chopsticks. He thought about the suggestion box note. What if Ronny knew he'd tattled? What would Ronny do?

Shawn heard Ronny laughing.

"Only sissies play violin," the mean boy said. "And only weirdos eat with chopsticks!"

Jason leaped out of his seat. "Leave Shawn alone!"

"It's not cool to make fun," Eric insisted.

Abby spoke up. "Eric's right. It's not cool." She was frowning.

Shawn was shaking.

"Have you ever heard of the Golden Rule?" Abby asked.

"Sounds dumb," Ronny said. He clumped around the table and stood behind Shawn.

Shawn could feel the heat.

"You can read about the Golden Rule in the Bible," Dunkum said.

Eric said, "Look it up. Matthew 7, verse 12."

Ronny laughed. "No thanks!"

Shawn wished Ronny would go away. His chopsticks were starting to rattle.

Ronny leaned over Shawn. "So . . . how was your chat with Miss Hershey?" he mocked.

Now Jason spoke up. "Get lost, Ronny Kitch!"

"Yeah," Abby said. "Or I'm telling!"

Ronny copied her in a pinched-up voice. "Or I'm telling!"

"I mean it!" Abby said. She got up and headed for the lunchroom teacher.

Shawn wished Abby would hurry back. He wanted her right here. With him.

Ronny stuck out his tongue at Shawn. "How do you like having your sister baby-sit you?"

Then he left.

Shawn put his chopsticks down.

"Ronny's rotten," Jason said.

Eric agreed. "No kidding."

Shawn looked up to see Abby coming back to their table. *Good*, he thought.

"Thank goodness, Ronny's gone," Abby said. She looked at Shawn. "And I think I know who started the nickname."

Shawn said nothing.

"It was Ronny," Abby said. "I'm right, aren't I?"

Shawn felt hot.

He pressed his lips tight.

SIX

The lunchroom was almost empty.
The Cul-de-sac Kids were still talking.
Abby said, "We can help you, Shawn."
Eric and Jason nodded.
"Abby's right," Jason said.
Dunkum and Stacy looked worried.
"Please tell us," Stacy said.
Finally, Shawn said, "I not want trouble."
"Who does?" Jason said. "But Ronny Kitch is already trouble."
"Big trouble," Eric said. "He pushed

me around during recess. I had the ball. I was dribbling, close to making a goal."

Shawn listened. Anything about soccer, and he was all ears.

"I was ready for a kick to the goal," Eric continued. "But the ball got jerked away. By guess who?"

Jason was wide-eyed. "Ronnie is NOT a team player!"

Eric nodded. "That's the truth."

"And he was on *your* team," Jason said.

"That's the weirdest thing," Eric said. Shawn listened.

"What happened next?" Abby asked.

Eric's eyes rolled. "Ronny booted the ball. *He* made the goal."

"It should've been yours," Jason said.

"That's how Ronny is," Eric said. "Rotten."

Shawn's jaw twitched. "That not how things be," he said. "Must change!"

Abby's eyes were on him now. "We

need to have a long talk," she said. "How about after school?"

"I play violin then," he said.

"How about when you get home?" Abby asked.

Jason smiled. "Good idea. Talk to Abby. She's a good listener."

"Good friend, too," said Stacy. "Chingu." She smiled at Shawn.

But Shawn was silent.

★ ★ ★

The Cul-de-sac Kids went out for recess.

Abby and Stacy scurried off to the swings.

Dunkum and Eric went to shoot hoops.

"Wanna play soccer?" Jason asked Shawn.

"Thank you, but no," he answered.

"Aw, come on," Jason said. He looked at the soccer field. "Ronny's not playing."

Shawn checked things out. Jason was

right. Ronny was way on the other side of the playground.

It was safe.

"Come on," Jason insisted. "I'll teach you."

Shawn didn't need to be taught. But Jason didn't know that.

Jason begged him to play. "Come on, you'll love it," he said. "I know you will."

Shawn really wanted to play. This would be his first chance to play on the field. The long, beautiful soccer field.

He glanced at the far end of the playground. Ronny was still there.

At last, Shawn agreed. "OK, I play."

Jason started by showing how to dribble. A little at a time.

Shawn dribbled, too. But he kept watch for Ronny.

Jason showed how to rocket the ball to the goal.

Shawn tried. Three times he made it.

Jason shouted, "Goal!" each time.

Shawn was having a great time.

He forgot about Ronny.

"Wow, you're good," Jason said. "Did you play soccer in Korea?"

Shawn grinned. He didn't want Jason to know about his secret practice. "Not play in Korea."

Jason seemed surprised. "Let's try some fancy moves."

"I try," Shawn said.

Jason grinned and showed off his fancy footwork.

Shawn was getting the feel of it. He was doing really well.

Suddenly, a shadow fell over him. An enormous shadow. The shadow followed the ball as it rolled downfield.

Jason yelled at the big shadow. "Hey! We had the ball first!"

But Shawn didn't say anything. He kept dribbling. There was no other choice. It was dribble or die.

The shadow was roaring now.

Too close!

43

SEVEN

Shawn raced toward the goal area. He still had the ball.

"Fiddlesticks don't play soccer!" the shadow yelled.

Shawn tried to shut out the horrible nickname.

Fiddlesticks.

The name burned like red peppers.

Shawn couldn't think about the ball. He couldn't think about his feet. And the goal—which way was the goal?

"Fiddlesticks . . . fiddlesticks!" the voice shouted.

Shawn knew that voice. It was the put-down voice. That voice kept him awake at night. Sometimes, he heard it in his worst dreams.

Shawn turned around slowly.

Ronny rushed at him like a giant. "Go back where you came from," he sneered.

But he kept coming.

Closer.

Shawn was scared stiff. He sped up.

"Don't you understand English, fiddlesticks boy?" Ronny said. "Go back to Korea! I don't want you here!"

Jason caught up. "That's a horrible thing to say."

Ronny stopped running. He turned and looked Jason in the eye. "Don't stick up for fiddlesticks!" Ronny roared.

"Stop it!" yelled Jason. "Shawn's not fiddlesticks! He's a *person*!"

Shawn stopped running. He stood very still. He saw the angry glow in Ronny's eyes and was afraid for Jason.

45

Ronny put up his fists.

Shawn gulped. "Not fight!" he shouted. "Please, not fight!"

Ronny glared at Shawn. "Keep out of this! You got me in trouble with Miss Hershey. You'll be sorry for that!"

Then Ronny spotted the soccer ball. He shoved Jason aside. He charged down the field toward Shawn.

Zoom!

With a mighty kick, the ball flew across the field.

Ronny roared like a lion. He dribbled a few feet downfield. Then he booted the ball toward the goal.

But the kick was off. Way off. It landed out of the line.

Jason started laughing.

Shawn didn't. He was too scared.

Just then, the recess bell rang.

Jason pulled on Shawn's shirt sleeve. "Let's get out of here."

Shawn's face was burning. "You not

fight. That good thing."

"*This* time Ronny was lucky," Jason muttered. "I wanted to smash his face."

The boys hurried to the classroom door. They huffed and puffed.

Shawn looked back over his shoulder. Jason looked back, too.

"Ronny not coming," Shawn said.

"That was close," Jason said. Then he wiped his face on his sleeve. "Hey, you're really good. You should come practice soccer after school. After violin."

Shawn wanted to. He really did. But Ronnie Kitch might be there.

Should he take the chance?

EIGHT

Ronny bugged Shawn all afternoon. He poked him with a pencil. He kicked his chair. He muttered put-downs.

"You told about the nickname," Ronny whispered. "Miss Hershey scolded me at lunch."

Shawn thought Miss Hershey's talk would change things. But it hadn't. Ronny was still pestering him.

Now Miss Hershey wasn't looking.

Ronny whispered again. "Better watch that dumb violin of yours. It might disappear!"

Shawn curled his toes inside his shoes. Ronny was rotten. Was he a thief, too?

Shawn didn't want to sit near Ronny anymore. He couldn't think about his work. He couldn't think about his violin lesson. And he couldn't think about something else. Trying out for soccer!

★　★　★

After school, Shawn's violin teacher greeted him. "How's it going, Shawn?" asked Mr. Jones.

"I have big surprise," Shawn said.

Mr. Jones's eyes lit up. "What's the surprise?"

"I learn all songs for you," Shawn said.

He tucked his violin under his chin and began to play.

Mr. Jones closed his eyes. He swayed to the music. Sometimes he stopped to point out soft and loud parts.

When Shawn finished, Mr. Jones smiled. "What a wonderful surprise. You are an excellent violin player."

Shawn bowed low. He wanted to bow—
even in America.

After his lesson, Shawn hurried to the
soccer field. He looked for Jason and Eric.
They were nowhere in sight. Ronnie Kitch
was. Right in the middle of everything.

Quickly, Shawn turned away. He
gripped his violin case and remembered
what Ronny had said. *Better watch your
violin.*

"No soccer for me," Shawn said out
loud.

"Why not?" a voice called.

Shawn spun around.

It was Jason Birchall.

"Hi," Shawn said. He was glad to see
his friend.

"You're staying, aren't you?" Jason
asked.

"Well . . . uh . . ." Shawn looked down
at his violin. He wanted to stay and play
soccer. He really did. But he didn't want

to lose his violin. His wonderful, beautiful instrument. Ronny might steal it out from under his nose!

Just then, Coach spotted Shawn. "Welcome!" he called and kicked a ball to him.

Shawn stopped the ball with his foot. But he held on to his violin case.

"Come on!" hollered Jason. He was already running down the field.

So was Coach.

Shawn dribbled around the edge of the field. Far away from Ronny. His violin was safe with him.

He punted back and forth with Jason. Then he rocketed the ball toward the goal.

"Hey, good stuff!" hollered Jason.

Now Eric was there, too. "Glad you showed up," he said. Then he stared at the violin. "Why are you carrying your instrument around?"

Shawn ran to get the ball.

Jason called to him, "It's not a good

idea. Your violin might get crunched."

Shawn thought about it. He loved his violin. He was good at it. The music made him feel terrific.

"I keep violin with me," Shawn said. He held up the case and grinned. "I run with music."

Suddenly, Ronnie was coming at him. Fast!

Shawn didn't have time to protect his violin.

He closed his eyes and prayed.

His violin was about to be history.

So was he!

NINE

Sa-whoosh! Ronny flew past Shawn.

"Fiddlesticks!" Ronny whispered into the wind.

Shawn heard the nickname. He almost dropped his violin case. He gripped harder.

Seconds later, Ronnie turned around. He charged at Shawn again. "Fiddlesticks never play soccer!" he hissed.

Shawn wanted to bop him. Flatten him good!

But the nickname mixed him up. He

couldn't remember what to do with his feet.

His ball spun away. It was loose at midfield.

Ronny laughed. "Fiddlesticks boy!"

Shawn was still carrying his violin. He looked down. He thought, *This case very hard. Make good head bopper.*

He scanned the field. The coach was at the other end—out of sight. He would never see Ronny getting bopped!

Shawn raised his violin case. His heart thumped.

"Don't!" yelled Eric from the goal.

Ronny punted a ball off his head. "You'll be sorry if you hit me!" he shouted at Shawn.

Ka-boink! Ronny's ball bounced off Shawn's violin case. On purpose.

Shawn saw Eric dashing toward him. "Don't fight back!" Eric yelled. "Remember the Golden Rule."

Just then, Coach came running. He

nabbed Ronny. He lugged him right off the field.

Ronny roared and ranted.

Jason laughed. "What a big baby!"

Shawn agreed, but he didn't say anything. He felt awful. He'd almost hit Ronny.

He'd come so close.

★ ★ ★

At home, Shawn and Abby had a long talk.

Abby read Matthew 7:12 out loud.

"Read very slow," Shawn said.

Abby did. " 'Do for other people the same things you want them to do for you,' " she read.

"Gold rule?" Shawn asked.

"The *Golden* Rule," Abby told him. "The most important rule of all."

Shawn thought about the Bible verse. He thought about Ronny Kitch.

"Ronny not know rule?" he asked.

56

Abby shook her head. "I doubt it."

"I teach," Shawn said. "I teach Ronny Golden Rule."

Abby looked surprised. "What do you mean?"

"You see," Shawn said.

"Be careful around Ronny," Abby said. "He could easily beat you up."

"I get strong body," Shawn said. He stood up. "And you help me."

He went outside. Abby followed.

"I be strong. No more fiddlestick legs. No more jelly bean muscles," Shawn explained.

He knelt down in the grass. He started with push-ups. Next, came sit-ups. Shawn ran around the backyard while Abby timed him.

"Now measure," Shawn said. He wanted Abby to see if his arms were bigger. His legs, too.

Abby found the measuring tape.

He hadn't grown.

The second day, Shawn ran and jumped some more. He did twenty sit-ups. He groaned through fifteen push-ups.

Abby measured his muscles. "No change," she said.

Every day Shawn did his exercises. For two whole weeks!

He ate more food than usual. More American food, too. Pizza and cheese-burgers.

Ice cream and cake.

And lots of celery with gooey dips.

The day before soccer tryouts, Abby measured Shawn's muscles. "They're the same size," she said.

Shawn frowned. "What go wrong?"

Abby tried to explain. "Building up your body takes time. Two weeks isn't enough. Keep exercising."

Shawn sat on the porch step. His face drooped. "I still fiddlesticks. I always be fiddlesticks."

"That's not true!" Abby sat beside him.

"You're Shawn Hunter. Don't call yourself fiddlesticks anymore!"

Shawn was quiet.

So was Abby.

Brr-eep! A cricket chirped.

Buzz-za biz-z-z. Bees hummed.

At last, Shawn said, "Maybe I supposed to be small."

"Small isn't so bad," Abby said.

Then Shawn had an idea. "I be fast! Fastest small person in world!"

Abby grinned. "That's a double dabble good idea."

"Tomorrow, I be fastest player on soccer field!"

Shawn couldn't wait for tryouts.

TEN

That night, Shawn packed away his chopsticks.

"I use fork now," he said at supper. "I live in America."

Abby smiled.

So did the rest of the family.

After supper, Shawn helped Abby load the dishwasher. When they were finished, he asked her to pray. "I want God to help."

"About making the soccer team?" Abby asked.

Shawn nodded. He pointed to himself.

"About skinny body, too."

Abby smiled. "God won't make you big overnight."

Shawn frowned. "I *need* big, power body."

Abby said, "God makes our bodies grow. But we can't be in a hurry."

"Shawn in very big hurry," he said.

"Be happy with who you are," Abby said and looked at Shawn. "But I'll pray about tryouts."

Shawn's eyes shone. "I like that. Very much!"

Abby prayed. At the end she said, "Amen."

"Amen, too," Shawn said. "I go now. Thank you for prayer."

He went to his room. There, he took out a picture. He sat on the floor beside his dog. Snow White nuzzled into his lap.

Shawn's Korean parents were in the picture. He studied it.

"Father not have power body," he said.

Just then, Jimmy, his little brother, came in.

Shawn hid the picture behind his back.

Jimmy found his skates and left.

Shawn sighed. He looked at the picture again. He missed his parents. His father had died years ago. Then his mother became sick. She couldn't take care of Shawn and Jimmy anymore.

Shawn put his arms around Snow White and she licked away his tears.

Shawn hugged the dog. "You very good pet," he said. "You Golden Rule dog!"

ELEVEN

It was Friday. Soccer tryouts day!

Shawn got up early. He took a warm shower.

Before he dressed, Shawn measured his arms. He hadn't grown overnight. No power body.

Abby was right.

But Shawn knew he could be fast. Faster than the other boys. Even faster than Ronny Kitch!

★　★　★

Freeet! Coach blew his whistle.

The boys lined up.

"Show me some teamwork," Coach said.

Jason, Eric, and two other boys burst onto the field.

Shawn watched eagerly. They did lots of passing and shooting. Back and forth.

He waited his turn, holding his violin. He didn't dare put it down. Not with Ronny around.

Just then, Ronny came over. "Taking care of that stupid thing?"

Shawn didn't answer.

"Are you deaf, fiddlesticks boy?" Ronnie demanded.

Shawn paid no attention. He thought of the Golden Rule and fished out a candy bar from his pocket.

"You like?" Shawn held up the candy.

Ronny frowned at first. Then his eyes blinked. He snatched up the candy. "Give me that!"

And off he ran.

Shawn felt inside his pants pocket. He smiled. There was plenty more candy. He was ready for Ronny.

His plan was good. A golden plan.

"Shawn Hunter!" The coach called.

He was next.

The coach glanced at Shawn's violin. A thin smile crossed his face. Then he looked away.

One kid shouted, "Hey, look! Shawn's trying out with a violin!"

Coach waved his hand. "It's music month, right?"

Kids on the sidelines snickered.

"Teamwork!" yelled the coach. He blew his whistle again. "Heads up. Spread out."

Four players rushed onto the field. All of them wanted to be on the team. But none of them more than Shawn.

Things got off to a swift start. Shawn dribbled and passed rapidly. The others scrambled to keep up. Down the field they flew. Clutching his violin, Shawn eased in and out of the players.

"Go, Shawn, go!" Jason shouted.

Fast as he could, Shawn worked his way down the field.

His teammates shot the ball to him and he stopped it with his foot. He dribbled a few yards. He remembered Jason's fancy footwork. And tried it out.

He was approaching the goal area.

The goalie was guarding like a hawk.

Shawn had to trick him. How?

Teamwork, he thought.

Shawn passed to another player. That player dribbled to the left, then booted it back.

Shawn stopped the ball with his hip and took control.

Pow! He snapped a clean shot into the net.

"Goal!" someone shouted.

Kids chanted on the sidelines. "Go, fiddlesticks, go!"

The coach blew his whistle. Long and loud.

The crowd got quiet.

"Next group!" Coach said.

Tryouts were over for Shawn. He felt good about his passing and shooting. But mostly he felt glad about his speed.

Jason and Eric circled Shawn.

"You were great!" Jason said.

"He sure was!" Abby said, running up to them.

"You great, too," Shawn said to his cul-de-sac friends.

Eric scratched his head. "How can you play soccer and a violin?"

Shawn replied, "Not easy." He smiled so big his eyes winked shut.

Jason asked, "Hey, what were those kids chanting?"

Shawn tossed his head. He knew. It was the nickname.

"Something about fiddles, I think,"

67

Eric said. "Maybe that's because Shawn's so good at violin."

Abby wrinkled up her nose. "Just forget it, OK?"

"Fiddlesticks," Shawn offered. "Kids call me 'fiddlesticks.' "

Abby's eyes nearly popped.

Shawn shook his head. "Nickname not bother me now. Fiddlesticks good name."

Ronny looked their way. He didn't come barging over. But Shawn knew he'd heard what Shawn said.

"Ronny learn golden things," Shawn said softly.

Abby frowned. "What do you mean?"

Shawn thought about the Golden Rule. But he kept quiet.

The kids walked toward Blossom Hill Lane. They talked about soccer and the team list.

"When will we know who made it?" Jason asked.

"Monday, after school," Eric said.

"A whole weekend to wait," Abby chanted.

Jason jigged down the cul-de-sac. "Wouldn't it be cool if we all made the team?"

"Very cool," said Shawn.

But he was thinking about Ronny. Would *he* make the team, too?

TWELVE

Monday finally came.

The team list was posted high on the P.E. door.

Shawn stood on tiptoes, reading the bottom names first. He saw Jason's name. And Eric's.

Shawn kept going, reading *up* the list.

"Hey," called Jason. "Did you make the team?"

Shawn was still reading. "*You* make team," he said.

Jason started to dance in the hall.

Shawn made his eyes squint. But the names on the list were too far away. He couldn't see them.

The school bell rang. Kids hurried to class.

"Come on," called Jason. "We'll be late."

Shawn turned to go. He wished he could see the top names. Maybe his was up there.

Maybe not.

★ ★ ★

Miss Hershey called the roll.

After that, she passed around some papers.

Shawn read his right away. *Very good*, he thought. *Music homework.*

"We're going to do something special for Bach's birthday," Miss Hershey said. "We're going to have a Bach Bash."

Some of the kids had forgotten who Bach was. Miss Hershey reminded them of the famous music composer. Then she handed out ideas for creative reports.

Shawn raised his hand. "I play Bach piece on violin, yes?"

Miss Hershey smiled. "I hoped you would want to play," she said. "Thank you, Shawn."

All morning, Ronny was kind. He didn't poke Shawn. He kept his feet to himself. He didn't say the nickname.

The class got busy. They divided into groups. Ronny was in Shawn's group.

Miss Hershey came around and listened to each group. But Ronny was silent. He let Shawn do all the talking.

Shawn was surprised. What a big change.

It was a Ronny Kitch switch!

★ ★ ★

During recess, Shawn and Jason went to P.E. They looked at the soccer list.

73

Jason spotted Shawn's name. "You made it!" he cried.

Shawn jumped up to see his name. It was at the top of the list. But he kept looking. "I not see Ronny on list," he said.

Jason shook his head. "Ronny didn't make the team this year."

"He not?" Shawn asked.

"Coach heard about the nickname," Jason said. "He didn't like the way Ronny was acting."

Jason ran out for recess.

Shawn hurried to catch up, but inside he felt sad. Sad for Ronny.

Shawn played on the soccer field with the other boys. Ronny watched from the sidelines.

Then Shawn had an idea. Another golden one. He marched off the field. Right up to Ronny.

"You want candy?" he asked.

Ronny's face turned happy. "Are you

kidding? After what I called you? After what I did?"

Shawn gave him an eyeball gum ball. "For you from fiddlesticks."

Ronny's mouth dropped two feet. "What did you say?"

"You not deaf. You hear right," Shawn said. "Fiddlesticks nickname good. Make me run fast. Make me feel like music."

Ronny shook his head. "I don't believe this."

"Believe," Shawn said. "Good thing to believe."

He thought of the Golden Rule.

And he smiled.

THE CUL-DE-SAC KIDS SERIES
Don't miss #12!

THE CRABBY CAT CAPER

Dee Dee Winters is worried. Mister Whiskers has run away. The Cul-de-sac Kids help her search Blossom Hill Lane, hoping to find the crabby cat.

When Mister Whiskers is spotted at the school carnival, the cul-de-sac pets join the hunt. A wild chase!

Dee Dee sees her cat perched high in the top seat of the Ferris wheel. But something goes wrong—it stops! Poor Mister Whiskers meows and paws the air. Dee Dee holds her breath and covers her eyes.

Will the cranky kitty stay put till the fire truck arrives?

ABOUT THE AUTHOR

Beverly Lewis thinks nicknames can be fun. "But the mean kind are horrible," she says. And she remembers being teased. Even by a teacher! "I was as skinny as Shawn Hunter, and people made fun."

Playing the violin and piano were a big part of Beverly's life. Her violin training began in fourth grade. She played all through high school and college. Later, she taught violin and piano to many students.

But Beverly never played violin on the soccer field. Or carried it around for tryouts!

You will *always* laugh when you read The Cul-de-sac Kids series. The books are full of humor and mystery. Beverly loves writing kids' books—just for YOU!